Disney's
Mickey's Christmas Carol

This book was originally published in a slightly longer version.

A GOLDEN BOOK • NEW YORK

Golden Books Publishing Company, Inc., Racine, Wisconsin 53404

Poor Bob Cratchit! Mr. Scrooge had made him work late again—even though it was Christmas Eve. But now, at last, he could go home. "Merry Christmas!" he called.

"Christmas, bah!" shouted Scrooge. "Don't forget my laundry."

Bob lugged the heavy laundry bag through the icy streets. He stopped once to rest. When he thought of his family waiting for him, he trudged on.

"It's Papa!" Tiny Tim cried joyfully as Bob came through the door.

"Dinner will be ready soon," said Mrs. Cratchit, sighing. "I wish Mr. Scrooge would pay you more... He does have enough money."

But Scrooge *never* thought he had enough money. Tonight,
as always, he had stayed late at the office to count his gold.

His nephew, Fred, opened the door. "Here's a wreath for you,
Uncle," he said. "Come join us for Christmas dinner. We're
having roast goose and plum pudding and—"

"You know I *can't* eat that stuff!" shouted Scrooge.

"Give a penny for the poor?" asked a man out on the street.
"Give *that* to the poor!" cried Scrooge angrily, shoving the wreath over the man's head.

"All this Christmas fuss," muttered Scrooge. "Bah, humbug." He thought of his dead partner, Jacob Marley. "Marley never gave *anything* away," he said. "He was my kind of man."

At home, Scrooge sank into his favorite chair. He was just dozing off when—

CLANK, CLANK, CLANK!

Scrooge sat up with a start. The ghost of Jacob Marley was coming toward him.

"I was selfish," moaned Marley. "As I carry these chains through eternity, so will you, Scrooge."

"No!" said Scrooge. "It can't be. Help me, Jacob."

"Tonight," said Marley, "three spirits will visit you. Listen to them."

The ghost vanished. Scrooge shook his head. "I need rest," he thought. "Imagine—thinking I saw old Marley!"

He had barely fallen asleep when the alarm clock jangled. Scrooge opened his eyes and saw a fellow standing on the night table.

"I am the Ghost of Christmas Past," he said.

The ghost held out his hand. "I'll take you to a Christmas of long ago."

Scrooge and the ghost flew across the night sky to a house filled with music and cheerful voices. Scrooge looked in the window.

"Why, that's *me,* when I was young," he gasped. "There's old Fezziwig. He gave me my first job. And there's my lovely Isabel."

"You were happy then, Scrooge," said the ghost, "and full of love. But then you grew greedy and lost all your friends—even Isabel."

Scrooge turned away. "I don't want to see any more. Please, Spirit, take me home."

Ring! It was the alarm clock again. "I must have been dreaming," Scrooge said.

"Fee, fi, fo, fum!" boomed a voice. There was a giant sitting on Scrooge's chair, surrounded by a luscious-looking feast.

"What's all this?" demanded Scrooge.

"It's the food of generosity," said the giant, "something you know nothing about. I'm the Ghost of Christmas Present. Come! See what's happening tonight."

Scrooge peered through the cracked window of a tiny house. "It's the Cratchits!" he said. "What a poor dinner they're having. Why aren't they eating the food in the pot?"

"That's your laundry in the pot," said the giant.

"What's wrong with the lad?" asked Scrooge.

"Tiny Tim is very ill," said the giant. "He needs good food to make him strong and well. Pay his father more so he can buy his family enough to eat . . ." The giant's voice faded, and then he was gone.

Suddenly Scrooge was surrounded by thick clouds of smoke.

"I am the Ghost of Christmas Future," said a voice behind him.

Scrooge turned. "Whose lonely grave is this?" he asked.

"It belongs to a very rich man," said the ghost, "a man who was so selfish and unkind that he had no friends."

Scrooge read the name on the stone: "'Ebenezer Scrooge.'
This is *my* grave!"

"That's right," said the ghost.

"I don't want to die alone," cried Scrooge. "I'll change my
ways!"

"I'll change . . ." Scrooge's eyes flew open. He was at home. He was still alive—and there was still time to make a new beginning.

"It's Christmas morning!" he cried as he rushed outside.

He tossed bags of money to the men collecting for the poor.

"Hello, Fred!" he shouted when he saw his nephew. "May I still come to dinner?"

"Of course, Uncle," Fred replied.

"Splendid! I'll see you later. There's something I must do first."

A while later, Scrooge knocked at Bob Cratchit's door.

"Merry Christmas!" Scrooge said. "I have something for you."

"M-more laundry, sir?" Bob gulped.

Scrooge laughed. "Don't be silly, my boy!"

"Look, Papa," cried Tiny Tim, opening the sack. "Toys!"

"Friends are worth more than all the gold in the world,"
said Scrooge. "Cratchit, from now on you and your family will
have everything you need. Merry Christmas, my friends!"

"And God bless us every one!" shouted Tiny Tim.